MW00345319

POETRY FOR CHILDREN

FLAVORS FOR FRIENDS

BY JULIE ANN FAIRLEY
ILLUSTRATIONS BY LASHON T. HOLLINGTON

Flavors for Friends: Poetry for Children

Published by Collaborative Experience, Inc.
P.O. Box 341377
Jamaica, NY 11434
www.thecollaborativeexperience.com
collaborativeexperience@gmail.com

Library of Congress Control Number: 2020916820

Published in the United States

ISBN# 9781732840560

Copy Editor: Pittershawn Palmer
ankh@creativeankh.com
www.creativeankh.com

Book Cover and Inside Layout:
Karine St-Onge
www.shinyrocketdesign.com

DEDICATION

To all the dreamers, thinkers, movers and shakers!
There's nothing better than LOVE!

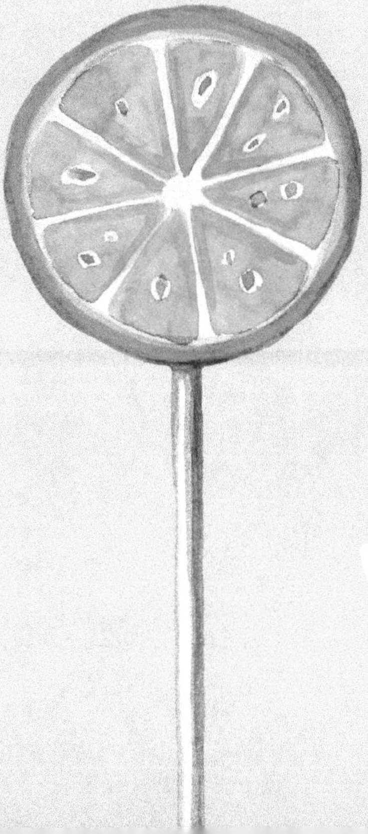

TABLE OF CONTENTS

Introduction 1

Poetry, That's Me 2

Want An Icee? 4

Anyway 6

I Am Not The Same 8

Things Are Possible 10

For Michelle (Michee) 11

Silence 12

Sunshine 13

Ooday Ooryay Ingthay 14

A Wonderful Spring Day 16

Where Is My Homework? 17

All I Can Be 18

My Animal 20

He's My Friend 23

Afraid 24
Life 25
I Can See A Rainbow 26
The Sound of Morning. 28
Best Friends 29
Geography 30
I Can't Help It 32
My Friend 35
He Said, She Said. 36
The Monster Hear – Say 38
Toe Tales 41
Write Me a Poem 42
Freestyle Facts Freestyle 44
About the Author 46

INTRODUCTION

My name is Julie Ann Fairley! Now I am all grown up!

I was born and raised in The Bronx, New York, the borough that is known as "The Boogie Down Bronx." In *Flavors For Friends*, I revisited many experiences and lessons I learned as a child.

I am the only daughter of Ms. Sadie Marie Applewhite. When I close my eyes, I can still hear her voice! "Julie Ann," she yelled as she stood in the front yard looking up and down the block for me. "Where in the world have you been?" Or, "Who is this you're bringing home now?" Or, "What did I tell you to do in the first place?" Or, "Didn't I tell you that everybody isn't your friend?" Or, "Where is your homework?" Or, "No...You can't go back outside." Or, "No...You can't have any company" and "No, You can't spend the night!" Or, "Don't ask me if she can stay for dinner because I can barely feed you." Or, "Girl, you better go somewhere and sit down!"

From what I have observed and learned in the classroom, as much as things change, many of our life lessons are still necessary and remain the same.

There is a common thread of situations and conflicts that children encounter. As a poet and writer, I felt the need to express myself and become the voice of love, joy, pain and sometimes anger for children of all ages. I have tapped into the little girl inside of me to write and share this book of poems. In her voice, I show children when an adult says, "I understand," there is truth in their words. The adult Julie Ann and the little girl, Julie Ann both love you!

POETRY,
THAT'S ME

I write poetry because my heart sings
Sometimes my heart aches
My soul stirs
Poetry sets me free!

I write poetry when breezes are cool
When raindrops form puddles that are splashed on my legs
When raindrops tap lightly on windowpanes
When music plays
When melodies make me shiver
I am poetry in motion

Aches, stirs, motion, FREE!
Poetry, that's me!
Sings – Free!
Aches – Free!
Stirs – Free!
Cool – Free!
Wet – Free!
Poetry, that's me!
Puddles – Legs!
Window – Panes
Music – Plays
Rainy – Days
Poetry, that's me!
Teardrops – Eyes
Love – Inside
Poetry, that's me!

WANT AN ICEE?

Ma...
Ma...
Mommy!
The hot sun is beaming down on my face
I look up at the window
Beamin'
Burning
Making me want something
Cold, freeze
Cold to drink
Cold to slurp on
Slurp, Slurp, Slurp!
Everybody outside pushin'
Tryin' to get to the icees
I need a quarter or a dime and some nickels
Ching, Ching, Ching
Change!
To make my cold dream
Cold thing come true
Ma...

Ma...
Mommy!
Stick your head
Under the shiny glass square
Come on Ma
Come on Mommy
Hurry!
The lady with the sweet, cold
Coco, Rainbow, Cherry, Mango
Smooth things
Ain't gon' wait too long
For me to get my Ching, Ching, Ching
Dimes and things
Silver and brown
Round
In my wet
Sticky hand
Ma...

Ma...
Mommy!
I stomp my foot on the hot ground
I yell
My throat is dry
I jump up and down
'Cause I need
Need
My cold thing
Coco, Rainbow, Cherry
Icee!
Mommy, PLEASE
Oops!
I forgot
My mind went somewhere
Empty headed girl!
Mommy ain't home
That glass up there
Is
Clear, clear
Empty!

ANYWAY

Daddy,
I loved you from the very beginning
When I realized I was me
There was you
'Cause Mommy said so
I loved you from the very beginning
And even though
You never came by to see me
And even though
You never called me
My dreams included you
My life stories included you
And I had pictures in my mind
Of all the possibilities of you and me
Once, I imagined you watchin' me jumpin' rope
Once, I imagined you takin' me shoppin'
Once, I imagined you coming to my school
And once, I imagined you
Pickin' me up and wipin' my bloody face after Lenny
Accidently
Hit me with the baseball bat
Pictures in my mind
All the possibilities of you and me

Daddy,
I loved you from the very beginning
When I realized I was me,
Listening to all of Mommy's once in a while stories about you
I felt good, Anyway
My Daddy
Knows there's me
My Daddy has to be

Busy
Very busy
And even though
You never sent me a birthday card
And even though you missed every graduation
And even though
Andre Bennett
Beat the daylights outta me in the school yard
And even though
Melvin gave me a black eye and took my money
My hopes for tomorrow included you
My prayers for better days included you
And I had pictures in my mind
Of all the possibilities of you and me

Once, I imagined you tellin' those wild boys not to bother me
Once, I imagined you at the cook out
Once, I imagined you cookin' breakfast
And once, I imagined you pickin' up the phone to call me
Pictures in my mind
All the possibilities of you and me
Daddy,
I loved you from the very beginning
ANYWAY

I AM NOT THE SAME

I'm not the same
I'm not like you
Look at my face, my hair
My lips, my shoes
I laugh funny --- HEE, HEE, HEE!
I walk funny -----as you can see
I play around though
I like to have fun
I like music, movies, video games
And then some
I love pizza and candy
I love ice-cream and cake
I love going to parties
I love walking around
Getting wet in the rain

I'm not the same
I'm not like you
My heart's been broken
By lots of people, SHOOT!
They laugh at me because I'm different or new
They chase me and hurt me too
They try to take the money I've saved
What they don't know
Is that I work EVERYDAY!
I help Old Man Beemo
From around the block
We collect bottles and cans
He shares his stuff
In class it's hard
Sometimes I can't read
Sometimes things get mixed up
Then you laugh and you tease
Sometimes numbers, signs
Division and percent
Probability and fractions
Don't make ANY sense
My writing is a mess
The work is often hard
But hey, that's me
I guess I'm pretty odd
I'm not the same
I'm not like you
Look at my face, my hair
My lips, my shoes
Listen to the words
Yes, my heart does speak
I try not to feel lonely
While you call me GEEK or FREAK
Or just beat me up
Whenever you can

I'm not the same
I'm not like you
Look at my face, my hair
My lips, my shoes
I stand right now
For you all to see
How my heart speaks
What's the matter with me?
What's the matter with me?
I'm not the same
I'm not like you
I look at myself and tell the truth
It's the right thing to do
I can draw and I can paint
I fix computers when they go on the blink
I can travel alone
On buses and planes
You don't even know how many countries I've seen
You don't even know how well I can sing!
So I'm here to say once again
I'm not the same
I'm not like you
Look at my face, my hair
My lips, my shoes
It's someone like me
Who is not the same
Who hopes they can bring about change
It's someone like me
Who is NOT the same
Who WILL bring about change

THINGS ARE POSSIBLE

Sunshine
and
blue skies
make me
feel good
When I
feel good
so many things are
possible
yo digo
cosas es possible en mi cabeza
y en mi corazon
cada dia y cada noche

FOR MICHEE
(Michelle)

Pretty girl
With the big brown eyes
They talk
Brown eyes
They dance
Lashes that flutter
You bat them and you don't even know it
Lashes that move
Pretty girl
With the big brown eyes
Sees it all!

SILENCE

The sound of silence
Gets me into my own thoughts
I want to rest
Take it easy
Do nothing except think
Close my eyes
Breathe,
Breathe,
Breathe,
Just take it easy

SUN SHINE

FOR TAWNIA MCCRAY

Hey!
You are Sunshine
You light up the world
You make me smile during dark days and cold nights
You make me warm
Sunshine
Sunshine
Shine!

OODAY OORYAY INGTHAY/ DO YOUR THING

(A fun poem in Pig Latin)

Ifhay, ooyay Auntway ootay ayplay Umcay out today---ay! Umcay out today---ay!	If you Want to play Come out today---ay! Come out today---ay!
Ifhay ooyay Auntway ootay ingsay Go and do your ingthay! Go and do your ingthay!	If you Want to sing Go and do your thing! Go and do your thing!

Ifhay ooyay
Auntway ootay anceday!
Music make me oovemay!
Music make me oovemay!

Ifhay ooyay
Auntway ootay aughlay
Go ahead and aughlay!
Go ahead and aughlay!

Ifhay ooyay
Auntway to unray
Move your legs and unray!
Move your legs and unray!

Ifhay ooyay
Auntway ahay endfray
Be one 'til the endhay!
Be one 'til the endhay!

Ifhay ooyay
Auntway ootay illchay
Sit down and be illstay
Sit down and be illstay

Ifhay ooyay
Auntway ootay Icray
Let it out and ighsay!
Let it out and ighsay!

Anceday
Ingsay
Go and do your ingthay!

Icray, Unray, Ighsay, Aughlay,
Anceday, Ingsay, Endfray, Illchay

Go and do your ingthay
Go and do your ingthay
Go and do your ingthay

Ootayayday!
Ootayayday!
Ootayayday!
TODAY!

If you
Want to dance
Music make me move!
Music make me move!

If you
Want to laugh
Go ahead and laugh!
Go ahead and laugh!

If you
Want to run
Move your legs and run!
Move your legs and run!

If you
Want a friend
Be one 'til the end!
Be one 'til the end!

If you
Want to chill
Sit down and be still
Sit down and be still

If you
Want to cry
Let it out and sigh
Let it out and sigh

Dance
Sing
Go and do your thing!

Cry, Run, Sigh, Laugh
Dance, Sing, Friend, Chill

Go and do your thing
Go and do your thing
Go and do your thing

Today!
Today!
Today!
Today!

A WONDERFUL SPRING DAY

Once on a spring day I saw lovely flowers
They were so beautiful just as beautiful as can be
But the rain looked down and said "They must need me!"
The spring flowers were so happy they danced with glee
That's what happened on a wonderful spring day

WHERE IS MY HOMEWORK?

You know you ain't got it
Didn't think about it
Went without it
Lost it
Could not find it
Too tired
Wasn't reminded
Left it
Little brother tore it
My sister destroyed it
Juice spilled on it
You know you just ignored it!

ALL I CAN BE

I have to be
All I can be
'Cause someone sacrificed so much for me
I have to work
As hard as I can
So the ones behind me will understand
I have to work and do
All that I can
'Cause someone before
Had a dream in their hands
I have to be
All I can be
'Cause someone who's watching may follow me
I have to listen
I have to think
I have to try
Can't give up and sink
I have to ask questions
When I am confused
Can't sit and pretend
That everything is cool

I have to look deeply
I have to decide
To do the wrong things or to do what is right
I have to take time
A few minutes each day
Be still, just listen to what my heart has to say
I have to be
All that I can
That will show
How much I love me
And when I love me
Is when I can love you
When that love is shown
There's much we can do
I have to be
All I can be

There's so much to see
There's so much that we
Can dream (clap, clap)
Can do (clap, clap)
Can work (clap, clap)
You too
I have to be
All I can be
All I can be
All I can be
All (clap) I (clap) can (clap) be (clap)
All I can be!

MY ANIMAL

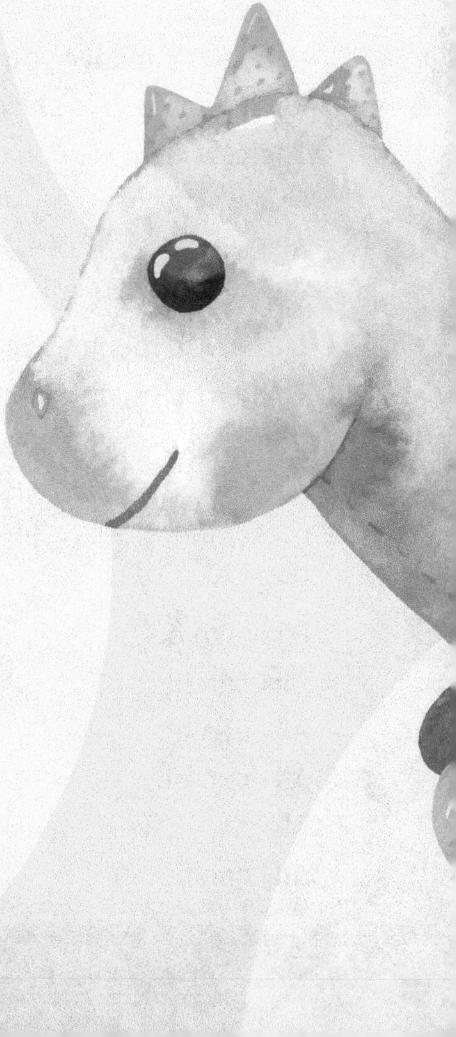

My animal is friendly
My animal is rough
It doesn't ask for anything
I don't give it much

It's lots of different colors
It's kind of fuzzy too
There's two black dots in its head
That stare right at you

My friendly, fuzzy
Wuzzy, wuzzy
Colored bubby
Is just enough
So I hold it
Then I rub it
And I'm glad that it is STUFFED!

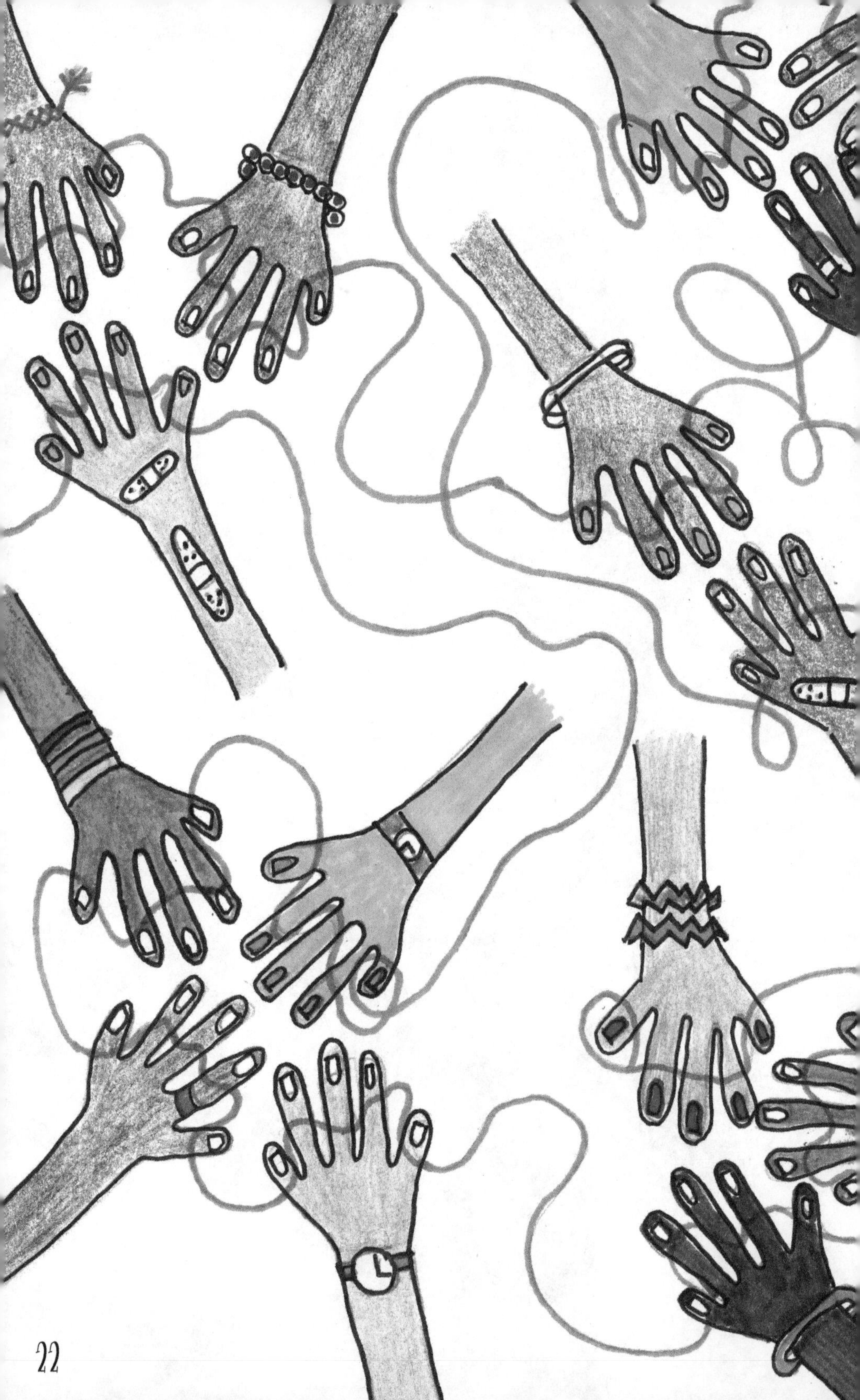

YEAH, HE'S MY FRIEND

Yeah,
He's my friend
He's silly and some might call him bad
Yeah,
He's my friend
He's crazy
There's some who he makes mad
Yeah,
He's my friend
He fights and stays in trouble too
But when I say I need him,
There's nothing he won't do
When I don't have any money
Or any place to go
He'll hang around with me
And share what he has too
He doesn't always do his homework
Sometimes he does tell lies
We sometimes get in trouble
But that comes as no surprise
Yeah,
He's my friend

AFRAID

I
used to be scared
afraid of
the night
and sounds that were
not familiar
when Mommy wasn't home

I
used to be afraid
scared of
the kids who chased me
and laughed at me
just because
they could

I
used to be frightened
afraid of my own thoughts
afraid of the places they might
lead me
afraid
I couldn't get out of my own skin

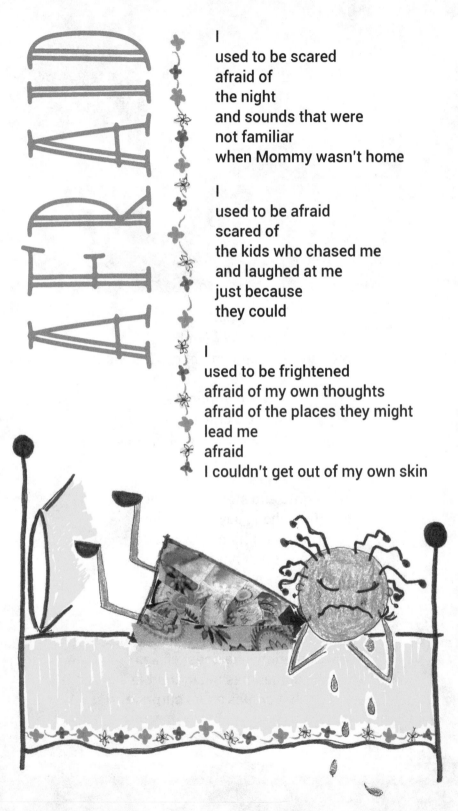

LIFE

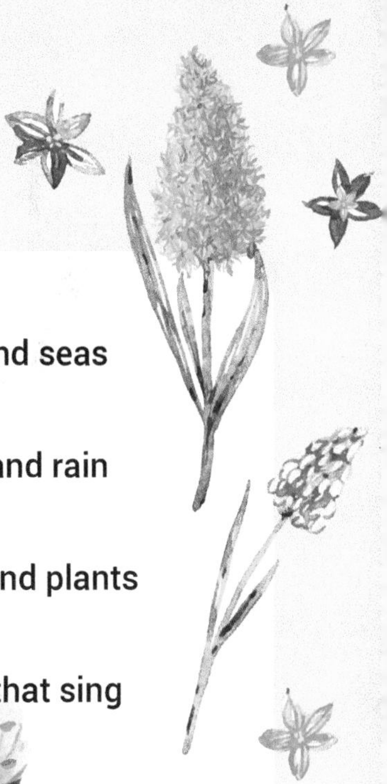

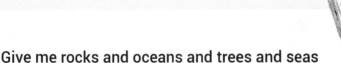

Give me rocks and oceans and trees and seas
Seeds and birds that fly

Give me stars and moons and clouds and rain
Thunder that roars up high

Give me lakes and rivers and flowers and plants
Grass that's oh so green

Give me music and dance and people that sing
Life,
What a wonderful thing!

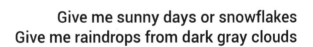

Give me sunny days or snowflakes
Give me raindrops from dark gray clouds

Give me honey dipped or ice-cream whipped
cookies, pizza, or pie

Give me strong warm breezes and ocean scents
Wet sand right under my feet
Give me music and dance
People that sing
Life,
What a wonderful thing!

I CAN SEE A RAINBOW

Red and yellow and pink and green
Purple and orange and blue
I can see a rainbow, do you?
I can see a rainbow, too!

Red and yellow
Colors so alive
Pink and green
Speak softly to the eyes

Purple and orange
Are lovely any day
Blue is the color that makes me want to say
I'm happy, I'm sad, I'm cool, I'm glad
In a funny sort of way

Yellow is the color that makes me wanna do
Some laughin' and singing and dancin' around too!
I can see a rainbow
The colors are on my mind
I can see a rainbow
With colors so alive
I'm happy
I'm sad
I'm cool
I'm glad

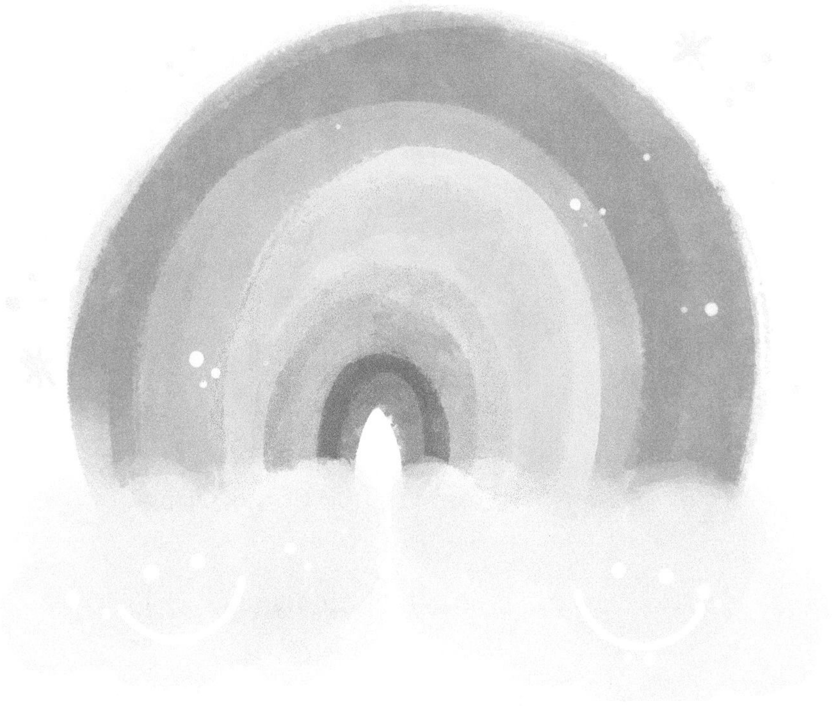

THE SOUND OF MORNING

I always loved the sound of morning,

Glory!

Birds chirping, birds flying,

Soaring!

Trees towering, caterpillars crawling,

Falling!

Creeks flowing, rain dropping,

Pouring!

I always loved the sound of the river,

Roaring!

I always loved the sound of the morning,

Glory!

Glory!

Glory!

BEST FRIENDS

Rough, tough
Had enough
Stop! No!
Let me go

Rough, tough
Knocked me down
Push and pull me all around

Rough, tough
They don't see
You're as gentle as can be
You're so funny and we laugh
I'm so glad you're in my class!

Rough, tough
Make me mad
I am stronger
You ain't bad!

Rough, tough
Let's go see
The world together
You and me!

Around the corner
Up the stairs
After class, ANYWHERE
Look at wrestling, basketball
Catch a football down the hall
We're just laughing having fun
All we want to do is run!

Rough, tough
I'm so glad
Best friend I could ever have
Ever have!

GEOGRAPHY

I'm North, I'm South
I'm round about
I'm East, I'm West
Don't know the rest
I'm somewhere in the middle
In a world that's far and wide
Could be Northeast
Could be Northwest
Could be Southeast
Could be Southwest

I'm somewhere in the middle
Wish I could tell you why

Maybe in the East
Maybe in the West
Guess I'm in the place
That I love the best
I'm somewhere in the middle
In a world that's far and wide

I'm somewhere in the middle
Wish I could tell you why

She came from over here
He came from over there
They all came from somewhere
'Cept I'm not sure just where

North, South, East, West
Over the mountains
And through the woods
Across the seas
In ships that stood
North, South, East, West
Latitude and longitude
Lines up, lines down
Lines that circle all around
Compass Rose and Legends too
Need all of those to locate you!

I'm North, I'm South
I'm round about
I'm someplace in the middle

In a world that's far and wide
I'm somewhere in the middle
Wish I could tell you why

North, South, East, West
Guess I'm in the place
That I love the best
See where you are and figure out the rest
You don't have to guess
You don't have to guess!

I CAN'T HELP IT

I was minding my business
Just standing alone
But the world is exciting
Like you didn't know!
There's so much to see
There's so much to tell
I can't help it if I
Can't keep it to myself

The trees, the bees, the birds, the flies
The lady, the man, the boys, the time,
The clothes, the shoes, the cars, the homes
Can't help it if I have to talk on the phone!
The girls, the secrets, the games, the fun
The jewelry, the music, the cutest one
The party
Who's coming? I'm going there too,
I'll tell you what I saw and you'll tell me too!
My cousins, my Tee-Tee, my family, my friends
My sister, my brother, my Uncle and them

I was minding my business
Just looking around
The world is exciting
Gotta share what I've found!

But I've gotta cool it
Can't be so surprised
When things go on and about in our lives

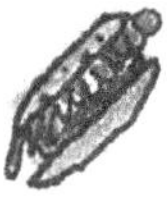

It's hard you see
Ooh! I can't help what I say
The world is exciting
Now they're calling me NAMES!

"You're so nosey,
Shut your mouth
Got so much to talk about!"

I can't help it
Is what I say
A wonderful world
It would be a disgrace
If I wasn't able to say what I say,
I just can't help it!

MY FRIEND

My Friend
I wanted you to be my friend
But then again
I shoulda thought about it first
Because
I really didn't know you

I wanted you to be my friend
You were new here
I smiled and welcomed you
I shoulda thought about it first
Because
I really didn't know you

I wanted you to be my friend
So you wouldn't have to walk home alone
I waited for you after school
Introduced you to my friends
But then again
I shoulda thought about it first
Because
I really didn't know you

I wanted you to be my friend
So we could call each other and laugh
About TV stars and candy bars and IPods
What we were gonna wear tomorrow
But then again
I shoulda thought about it first
Because
I really didn't know you

A friend begins deep within
It doesn't happen fast
'Cause often when it does
It really doesn't last
I wanted you to be my friend
But then again
I shoulda thought about it first
Because
I really didn't know you

We don't talk and we don't laugh
When we see each other
Neither one of us feels good

A friend begins deep within
It doesn't happen fast
'Cause often when it does
It really doesn't last

I wanted you to be my friend
But then again
I shoulda thought about it first
Because
I really didn't know you

HE SAID, SHE SAID

He Said, she said
You said and I said and he said, it's true
He said that she said, yes we said it too
They said that I said
Now that isn't right
You said that I said
Now they had a fight
She said that I heard that he said it after
That was last week
Now what does it matter?
You said that I said and he said it's true
He said that she said
Now what about you?
This sounds so crazy,
Confusing my mind
It happens so often and all of the time
She said and he said and they said it all
Now who said it really,
Who's really at fault?
He said and she said
What is her name?
She said that they said
Now who will we blame?
You said and I said and he said it's true
She said that he said
Now what about YOU?

TRASH

THE MONSTER HEAR-SAY

You better watch out for that monster!
You better watch out for that monster!
Monster Hear,
Monster Say

We're gonna tell you 'bout that monster,
We're gonna tell you 'bout that monster,

What we say
You know is true
The monster Hear-Say
Will come for you!

It makes you listen
It makes you laugh
It makes you smile
Will make you sad

It tells you things you didn't know
Tells you stories
And how things go

Will make you listen
Will make you smile
Will bring you trouble
In a little while

You better watch out for that monster!
You better watch out for that monster!

Monster Hear!
Monster Say!
Monster Hear!
Monster Say!

Don't pay attention to that Monster
Don't you listen to that Monster

Monster Hear!
Monster Say!
Brings so much trouble
Around the way!

Don't you listen or pay attention
Get caught up in a
Bad situation

You didn't hear
You cannot say
Don't bring that Monster
Around the way!

Monster Hear
Monster Say
Monster Go
The other way,
The other way!

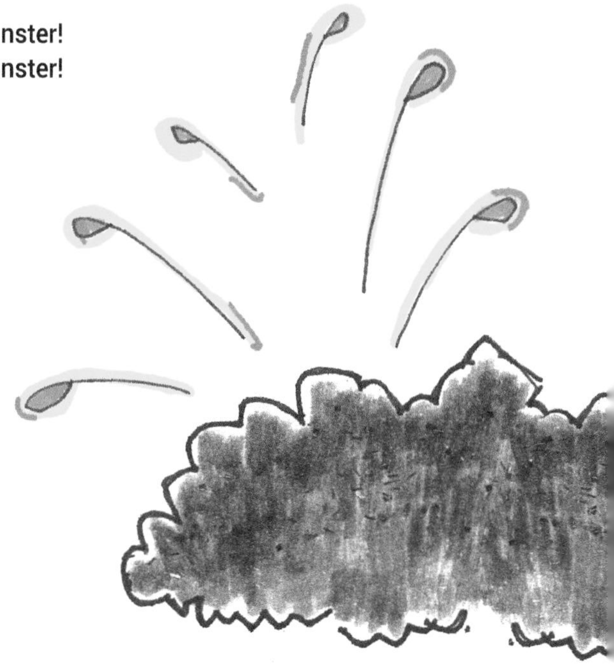

The Monster Hear-Say

BY

C. A. APPLEWHITE

KELSEY CITY FLORIDA

This life is a life of conflict,
Each moment and minute does fly,
But if you would have joy and sunshine
Just let old "hear-say" go by.

You may live in a palace of gladness;
Beneath the dark blue sky,
And then pay attention to old "hear-say
That Monster will make you cry.

Just, listen, I'll tell you a story;
A story of long ago;
When neighbors met neighbors of neighbor,
Their joy would overflow.

But these days, things are different;
Yes different I'll tell you so;
When some folks meet folks of some folks,
It's followed by trouble and woe.

Come and go with me ye people.
Upon mountains, plains and sea.
And crucify the monster hear-say,
Let's nail him to the tree.

Then your life will be full of singing,
While down life's stream you go,
Just keep your swords a-flinging.
Against that deadly foe.

" My poem, "The Monster Hear-Say" was inspired by my grandfather, Caiphas Applewhite who wrote about the same monster in his book of poetry in 1947."

TOE TALES

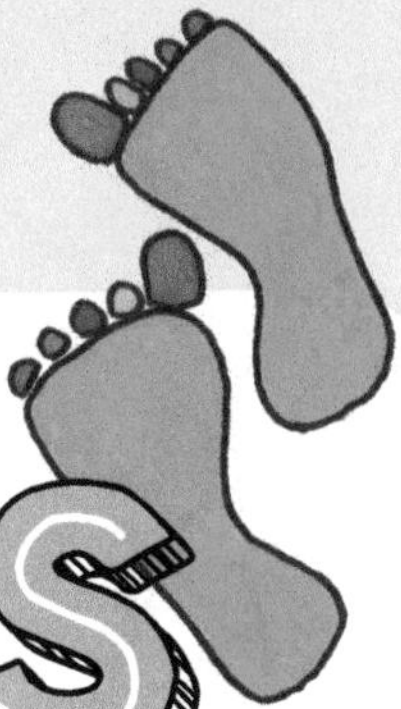

Everybody in the family has different toes

Jimboy's toes are long and skinny
He has big bumps on his pinky toes... He has corns.

Auntie V's toes are short and stubby... She has corns on top of corns almost looking like a piece of corn... Ooh! Look at her feet in the summer. She loves wearing white sandals and polishing her toenails bright red and putting white dots on them.

Brother D, My goodness! Uncle Ron told him to change his socks but he ain't listen so he got Whatchu call it? Whatchu call it? Athletes feet and all
His long brown toes smell like cheese and his toenails look like Whatchu call it? Whatchu call it? Sunflower seeds.

And my feet, my feet

Are big and pretty!

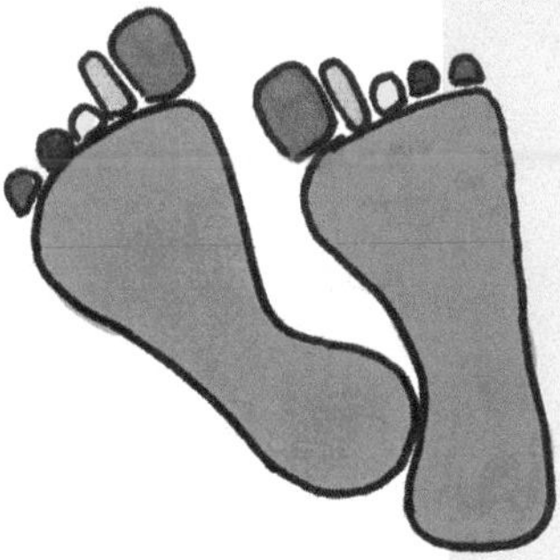

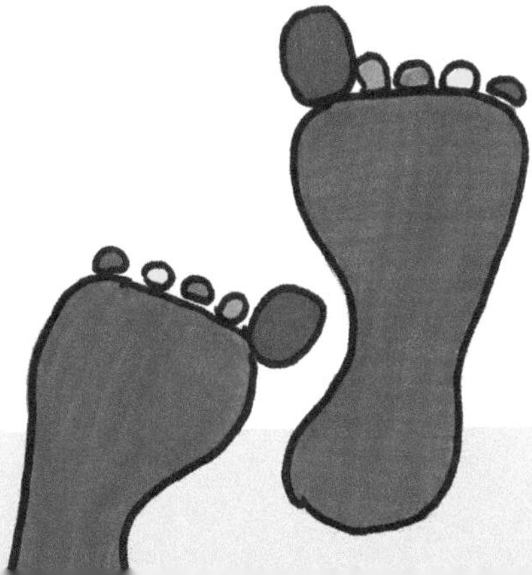

WRITE ME A POEM

I want you to write a poem
A Friday night poem
A she got on my nerves poem
An... I don't feel good poem
I want you to write a poem

An... I miss you poem
How about a hungry poem
Gotta get my life poem
An... I love my friends poem
An... I got dreams poem
Ain't got much money poem
A poem

I want you to write a poem
A cleaning up poem
A leave me alone poem
A house full of people poem
An... I need to breathe poem
I will make it happen poem
A poem

A listen to my song poem
An... I need a milkshake poem
A where's my homework poem
I want you to write a poem
An... I cry sometimes poem
An alone poem

An... I love my cousins poem
A what's in my heart poem
A love poem
A that's how we roll poem
Just write a poem

I want you to write a poem
An...I don't know what I'm doing poem
A leave me alone poem
Any poem
Find the words poem
Gotta be the best poem

A don't be ashamed poem
An... I don't care what they say poem
A this is me poem
A getting my life right poem

A making it happen poem
Not a trying poem
An...I'm doing it poem
JUST WRITE A POEM!

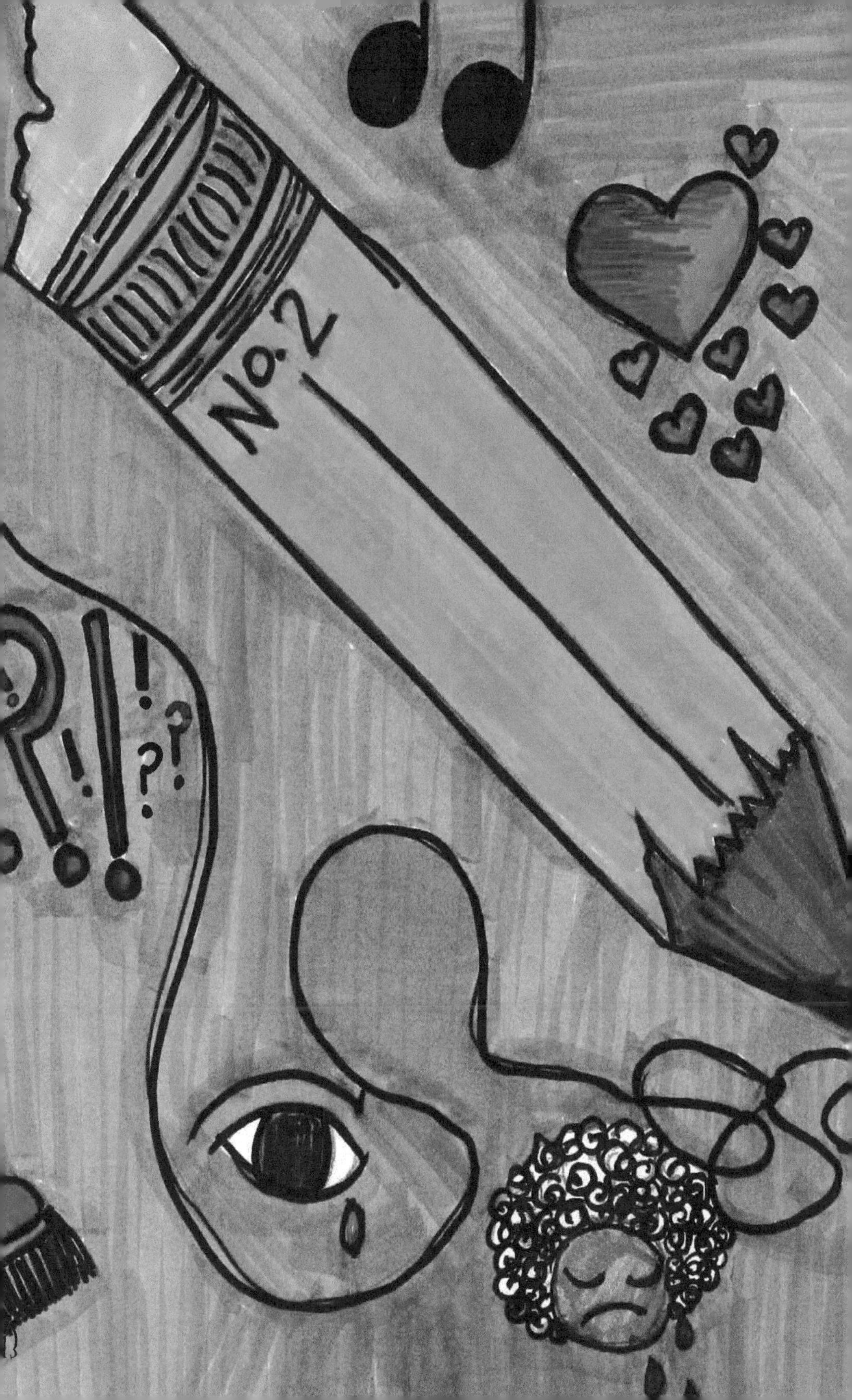
No.2

FREESTYLE FACTS FREESTYLE